Belle's Royal Wedding

By Thea Feldman

Illustrated by the Disney Storybook Artists

A Random House PICTUREBACK® Book

Random House 🏠 New York

randomhouse.com/kids

ISBN 978-0-7364-2993-1

MANUFACTURED IN CHINA

10 9 8 7 6 5 4 3 2 1

Belle and the Prince were going to be married in just a few days.

"I'm so happy!" Belle told Mrs. Potts. "The Prince has done so much for me. I want to make our wedding a special celebration to show him how loved he is."

"What a wonderful idea, my dear!" said Mrs. Potts as she hemmed the train of Belle's wedding gown. "I'm happy to help."

Belle thought back to how scared she was when she had first arrived at the castle. Everyone had been under a magic spell—the Prince was an angry beast, and all the servants were enchanted objects.

But over time, Belle became friends with
the servants, and she and the Beast fell in love.
Belle's declaration of love broke the spell!

Belle smiled at her friends. "I know you want to help with the preparations, but we also want you at the wedding as our guests. The Prince and I think of you as more than staff—you're family!"

The servants thought of Belle and the Prince as family, too. They worked hard to prepare for the big day. They wanted the happy couple to feel the love they put into every detail, from the cake to the tablecloths to the decorations.

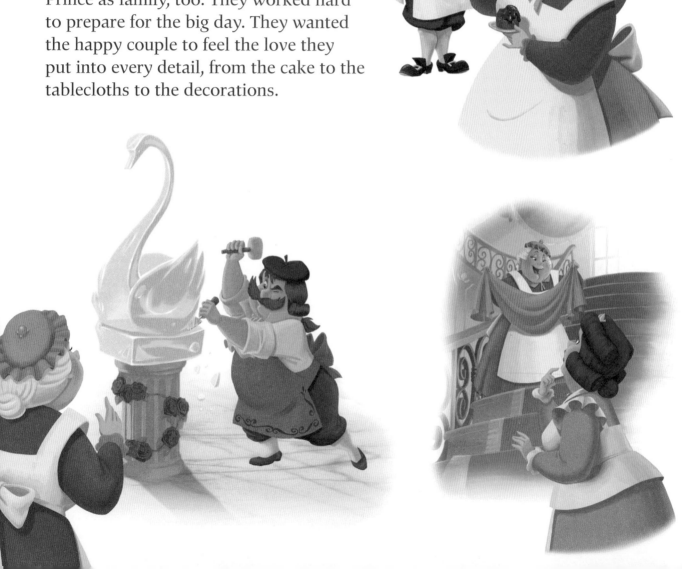

Meanwhile, the Prince was having a new suit made.

"I am the happiest man in the world!" he declared to Lumiere and Cogsworth. "And I want Belle to be the happiest woman! I need to find a special gift for her."

After the Prince left to go shopping, the servants started
planning a surprise for the young couple.

On the day of the wedding, everyone watched as the bride and groom promised to love each other forever.

Belle read from her favorite book of adventure stories. "But my greatest adventure is being with you," she told the Prince.

The Prince gave Belle his gift—a blank journal. "You can fill it with all the fun times we will have together!"

After the ceremony, Belle and the Prince walked into the ballroom. The servants had done a wonderful job!

"Thank you!" said Belle. "There's so much food, I don't think even our whole household can eat it all!"

Mrs. Potts and the other servants simply smiled and led the couple out to the patio. The entire village was there to surprise them!

"I took the liberty of inviting them, on behalf of the household," said Lumiere.

"Thank you for coming!" exclaimed the Prince over and over. Belle and the Prince couldn't stop smiling. They were thrilled to welcome everyone into their home.

"We are truly loved," Belle told her husband as they danced.

Fireworks lit up the night sky. Belle and the Prince knew their wedding had been a perfect celebration—for everyone!

As the sun began to set, the newlyweds rode off in their wedding carriage. "Best! Day! Ever!" Rapunzel cried out happily.

And they gave each other a bite of the wedding cake.

Flynn and Rapunzel danced their first dance as husband and wife while their friends looked on.

After a wild chase through the kingdom, the messy
ring bearers made it back to the ceremony just in time!

Rapunzel and Flynn were almost ready to take their vows.
Maximus and Pascal were still trying to catch the rings!

Flynn beamed when he saw Rapunzel.
She was a beautiful bride!

The wedding began. As the proud ring bearers walked down the aisle, Maximus sneezed—and sent Pascal and the rings flying through the air!

Luckily, Rapunzel didn't even notice. She kissed her father on the cheek and then turned to greet her groom.

On the morning of the wedding, bells rang throughout the kingdom, inviting all the townsfolk to celebrate. The streets were crowded with cheering, waving people as the King and Queen rode by in the royal carriage.

When it came time to choose the ring bearers, Rapunzel and Flynn knew just who to ask. Pascal and Maximus were thrilled to be part of the ceremony!

Next, Rapunzel looked for the perfect flowers. She didn't like any of the arrangements at the town's flower shop, so Tor helped her gather beautiful wildflowers from the fields.

After many hours, they finally created the most spectacular wedding cake Rapunzel had ever seen!

Attila and Rapunzel worked
together to design a wedding
cake. They baked and iced
and decorated, but they
couldn't get it quite right.

Flynn had just asked Rapunzel to marry him—and Rapunzel said yes! The happy couple couldn't wait to share the news with their friends. Everyone at the Snuggly Duckling was delighted and offered to help in any way they could.

Rapunzel's Royal Wedding

By Cian Spencer Carson

Illustrated by the Disney Storybook Artists

A Random House PICTUREBACK® Book

Random House 🏠 New York

randomhouse.com/kids

ISBN 978-0-7364-2993-1

MANUFACTURED IN CHINA

10 9 8 7 6 5 4 3 2 1